adapted by vick•e

designed by deborah boone

illustrated by jean-paul orpiñas and scott tilley

 A GOLDEN BOOK • NEW YORK

Copyright © 2008 Disney Enterprises, Inc. and Pixar. All rights reserved. Published in the United States
by Golden Books, an imprint of Random House Children's Books, a division of Random House, Inc., New York,
and in Canada by Random House of Canada Limited, Toronto, in conjunction with Disney Enterprises, Inc.
Golden Books, A Golden Book, A Little Golden Book, the G colophon, and the distinctive
gold spine are registered trademarks of Random House, Inc.

Library of Congress Control Number: 2007941169

ISBN: 978-0-7364-2422-6

www.goldenbooks.com

www.randomhouse.com/kids/disney

Printed in the United States of America

10 9 8 7 6

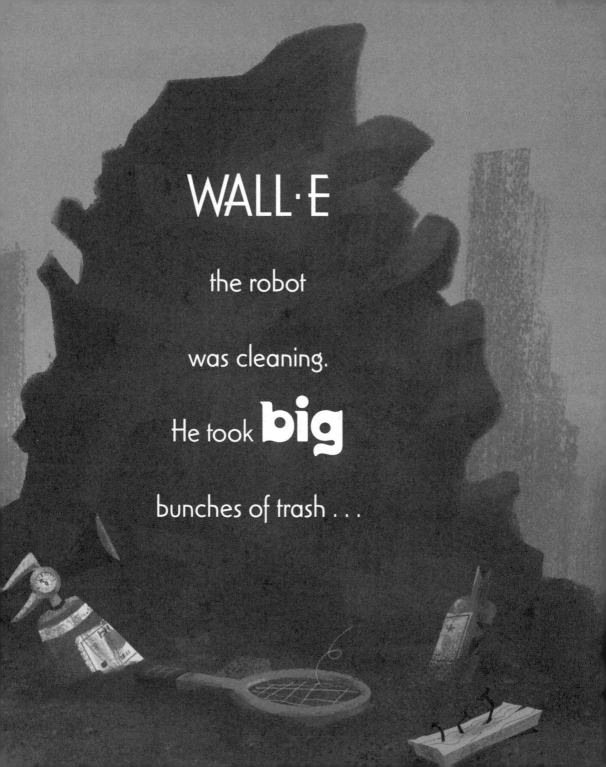

WALL·E

the robot

was cleaning.

He took **big**

bunches of trash . . .

. . . and compacted them
into cubes that were small.

He liked to find
fun things
in the trash.

whoosh!

He kept
the fun things
and cubed
the rest.

The best thing
he found
was a plant.

One day,
a spaceship arrived
and dropped off
another robot.

Her name
was EVE!

She was sent
to look
for something
special

It was a secret.

Shhhhhhhhh!

WALL·E had to make sure
that EVE was friendly.

At first, EVE did not seem friendly at all.

So WALL·E tried to follow EVE in secret.
Sometimes he was not very quiet.

clang! **clang!** clang!

But other times he was.

Eventually,
WALL·E and EVE
became friends.

WALL·E showed EVE the fun things he had collected.

He was hoping to hold her hand, but . . . EVE *grabbed* WALL·E's plant instead of his hand.

EVE fell asleep for a very long time. Then her spaceship returned to take her away!

WALL·E did not want her to go.

eeeeee!

WALL·E held on tight as the spaceship blasted into space.

He loved EVE and would follow her anywhere.

Soon WALL·E and EVE landed on a bigger ship. WALL·E kept following EVE.

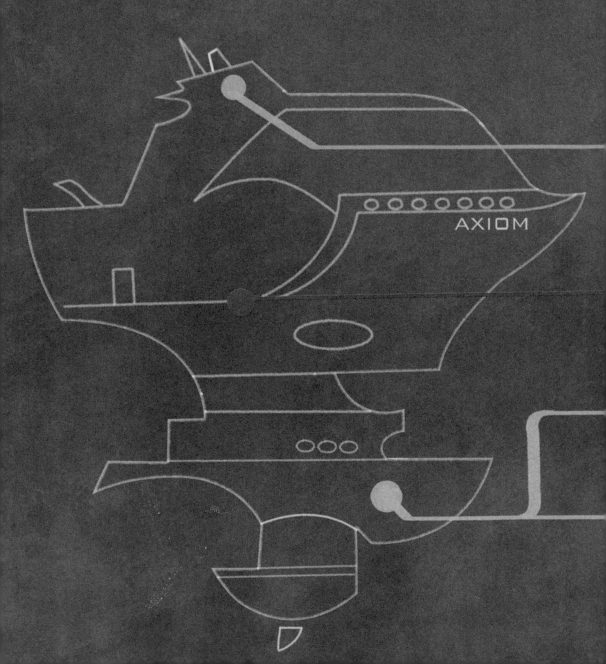

WALL·E **hid.**

WALL·E **met** new bots.

WALL·E **rescued** EVE.

Still, EVE would not hold his hand.

Then a bad robot zapped WALL·E.
He dumped WALL·E and EVE into the
garbage bay.

WALL·E gave EVE the plant. But now EVE
did not want it for her job. She wanted it
to help WALL·E.

EVE put the plant in
the ship's holo-detector
so that the ship could
go back to Earth.

EVE was happy
to see WALL·E's
home on Earth.
But she was sad
that he was hurt.

WALL·E needed EVE's help.
This time *she* rescued *him*.

And at last, WALL·E taught
EVE how to hold his hand.